WELCOME TO
PASSPORT TO READING
A beginning reader's ticket to a brand-new world!

Every book in this program is designed to build read-along and read-alone skills, level by level, through engaging and enriching stories. As the reader turns each page, he or she will become more confident with new vocabulary, sight words, and comprehension.

These PASSPORT TO READING levels will help you choose the perfect book for every reader.

READING TOGETHER
Read short words in simple sentence structures together to begin a reader's journey.

READING OUT LOUD
Encourage developing readers to sound out words in more complex stories with simple vocabulary.

READING INDEPENDENTLY
Newly independent readers gain confidence reading more complex sentences with higher word counts.

READY TO READ MORE
Readers prepare for chapter books with fewer illustrations and longer paragraphs.

This book features sight words from the educator-supported Dolch Sight Words List. This encourages the reader to recognize commonly used vocabulary words, increasing reading speed and fluency.

For more information, please visit passporttoreadingbooks.com.

Enjoy the journey!

Little, Brown and Company
Hachette Book Group
1290 Avenue of the Americas, New York, NY 10104
Visit us at LBYR.com

First Edition: July 2019

Little, Brown and Company is a division of Hachette Book Group, Inc.
The Little, Brown name and logo are trademarks of Hachette Book Group, Inc.

The publisher is not responsible for websites (or their content)
that are not owned by the publisher.

Library of Congress Control Number 2019932469

ISBNs: 978-0-316-49074-0 (pbk.), 978-0-316-49077-1 (ebook),
978-0-316-49078-8 (ebook), 978-0-316-49076-4 (ebook)

Printed in the United States of America

CW

10 9 8 7 6 5 4 3

Passport to Reading titles are leveled by independent reviewers applying the standards developed by Irene Fountas and Gay Su Pinnell in *Matching Books to Readers: Using Leveled Books in Guided Reading*, Heinemann, 1999.

OFFICIAL
MARK OF
SPIRIT

DREAMWORKS

Spirit

RIDING FREE

Lucky's Class Contest

by Jennifer Fox

Based on the episode
Lucky and the Competition Conundrum
Written by Katherine Nolfi

L B

LITTLE, BROWN AND COMPANY
New York   Boston

Attention, Spirit Riding Free fans!
Look for these words
when you read this book.
Can you spot them all?

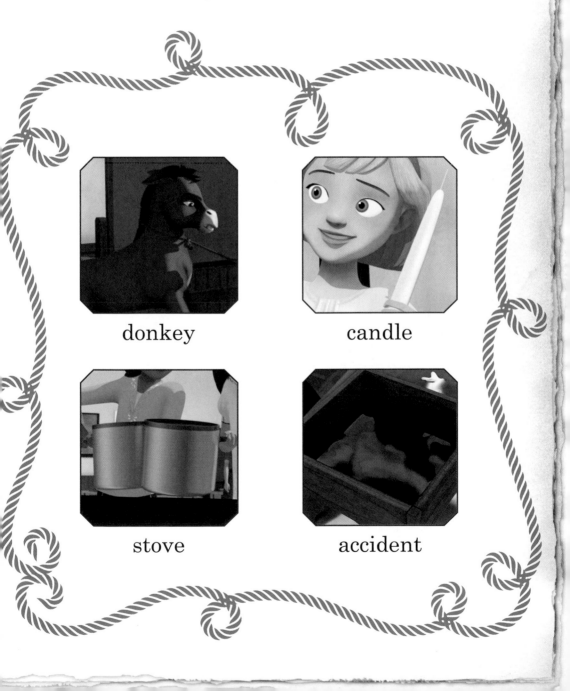

donkey

candle

stove

accident

Lucky runs into the classroom.
She is late to school again!

She arrives just in time
to hear Ms. Flores talk
about a special contest.

"You will work with one partner to create booths for our school fund-raiser," Ms. Flores says.

"The partners who raise the most money will be named the students of the month," continues the teacher.

Lucky wants to partner with one of her friends, but Pru and Abigail are already working together.

Lucky needs to find someone else to be her partner.

Snips says he wants
to be partners with
Señor Carrots.

Ms. Flores says he cannot do that
because Señor Carrots is a donkey.

Ms. Flores asks if Lucky
has found a partner yet.

Lucky does not think she
should work with Snips.

That leaves just Maricela!
"I am so glad we are
finally going to be a
team," she says to Lucky.

Later, Lucky, Abigail, and Pru
talk about the contest.
Lucky hopes she and Maricela
will be students of the month.

Pru and Abigail want
to win the contest, too.
"Ready for a little friendly
competition?" Lucky asks.
"You are on!" Pru replies.

Maricela says they have to work
hard if they want to win.

Lucky would rather ride Spirit
than work on the project.

Lucky goes to Maricela's house.

Maricela and Lucky have the
perfect idea for their booth:
a French café!

Pru and Abigail have
a good idea, too.
"We are making candles,"
Abigail says.

Maricela sees Lucky talking to
Pru and Abigail about the contest.

"Do not talk to them,"
Maricela says to Lucky.
"They are our competition."

The contest is bringing
out the worst in everyone.
Maricela bumps into Abigail
on purpose.

Abigail's horse-shaped
candle breaks!

Pru and Lucky fight for
space at the stove.

Lucky drops her hot chocolate
on the ground!

The night before the fund-raiser,
Lucky meets Maricela at the school.
She sees Maricela hiding
Pru and Abigail's candles.

"What are you doing?"

Lucky cries.

Maricela will do anything to win the contest!

Lucky tries to stop Maricela, but the candles fall on the floor and break!

"I have to fix them!"
Lucky shouts.

Lucky stays at the school
all night to fix the candles.

She is so tired that she
accidentally falls asleep!

Uh-oh.
Lucky has forgotten to take
the hot wax off the stove!

The candles melt
into a giant mess!

Ms. Flores wakes Lucky
the next morning.

"Lucky, what happened?"

Ms. Flores asks.

"It was an accident,"

Lucky explains.

Lucky feels awful and goes home.
"Do you think Pru and Abigail
hate me?" Lucky asks Spirit.

Later, Lucky explains
what has happened.
"We do not hate you!" Pru cries.
"You would never ruin our
candles on purpose," Abigail says.

At the fund- raiser,
Snips's dunking booth
is everyone's favorite.
He is the student
of the month.

The girls do not win,
but they do not mind.
Nothing beats being
friends forever!